A Polar Bear Night of Stars and Light

Written & Illustrated by Jennifer LaBella

Windermere House Publishing

Warmest wishes,
Jennifer LaBella

Published by
Windermere House Publishing
www.manitobabooks.com

ISBN 978-1-55383-204-1

LaBella, Jennifer, Author/Illustrator
www.landscapedesigner.net

A Polar Bear Night of Stars and Light

Printed and bound in Canada by
Friesens Corporation
One Printers Way
Altona, Manitoba, Canada, ROG OBO

The author would like to thank Robert R. Taylor, whose
expertise and guidance helped make this book possible.
Thanks also to Dr. Robert Wrigley for proof-reading
the manuscript, and to friends and family for their
encouragement and support.

A Polar Bear Night
of
Stars and Light

For Chloe

Foreword

The Arctic is facing some of the greatest challenges ever because of the rapid changes that have taken place in just the past 25 years. However, this situation is not irreversible. One of our best hopes is to inspire mankind about the importance of the Arctic and the magnificent beauty of Mother Nature's work.

Great artists have a unique ability to see life differently; their vision is a special gift to all of us. Jennifer LaBella is able to reach in and touch the souls of these animals and then bring them to life through her unparalleled talent. Her art allows us to travel with her and begin to understand the actual spirit of this place and its wildlife, leaving us with a determination to inspire others of the need to become better caretakers of this precious planet.

There is a strong chance that by the end of this book you will not be the same. The magic itself will change you, and hopefully, forever change our future.

Robert Buchanan, President
Polar Bears International
www.polarbearsinternational.org

Way up North,

where winters are long and cold,

two Polar Bear cubs lived with their mother.

She looked after them very well and they were a happy little family.

Each day, the cubs followed their mother

across the tundra toward the coast.

Soon they would head out to the frozen sea where the cubs would

learn to hunt for seals, the favorite food of Polar Bears.

Late one afternoon, soft white snowflakes floated down from the sky,
covering the ground in thick velvety drifts.

The cubs were having fun
tussling and tumbling in
the new-fallen snow.

While the cubs played,
the mother Polar Bear
dozed peacefully.

She was tired after long days of traveling over the hills and valleys of the tundra.

The cubs didn't notice
that the snow was falling
faster and faster.

When they stopped wrestling
and looked around, they couldn't
see their mother anywhere.

They must have wandered off while they were playing!

When the cubs began to search for their mother,
they noticed a white shape near a thicket of willows
and went closer to investigate.

An Arctic Hare, sitting motionless, jumped up
and bounded away across the snow.

As the hare disappeared from view
the cubs saw a pair of dark eyes
looking at them.

It was not their mother, but an Arctic Fox watching them
from behind a clump of spruce trees.

The fox gave a wide yawn
and trotted away.

Turning around, the cubs
glimpsed another white shape
on some rocks nearby, and
they crept up to investigate.

As they approached, a Snowy Owl turned its head
and stared at them with its big yellow eyes.

Ruffling its feathers, the owl leapt into the air,
spread its long wings, and flew off without a sound.

A snowdrift seemed to move,

　　　catching the attention of the Polar Bear cubs.

　　　　　Excitedly, they ran toward it.

All of a sudden, a flock of ptarmigan burst out of the snow,

　　　flying off in all directions.

It was beginning to get dark,
and the cubs still could not
find their mother.

The tired little bears nestled into a snowbank to rest.
Snuggling closely together, they imagined they were
safe and warm in their mother's thick white fur.

The cubs looked up at the night sky.
As the northern lights began
a colorful dance, a multitude
of tiny stars poked pin holes
through the darkness.

The cubs were amazed to see stars and lights

shifting into familiar shapes.

While they watched,

    the stars and lights transformed

        into an enormous Polar Bear!

Somehow,

  this beautiful twinkling bear

   reminded them of their mother.

The cubs felt she must be nearby. Comforted, they soon fell asleep.

A loud squawk of a Raven
echoed in the stillness.

At that very moment, the snowbank
in which the cubs were nestled,
started to move and shake. Snow flew everywhere!
It was the mother Polar Bear!
She had become blanketed in snow while she slept!

Happy to have found her at last,

the Polar Bear cubs settled down

for the night with their mother.

For a long time, they watched the beautiful starlit bear's silent march across the sky.

When their eyes could stay
open no longer,
the cubs drifted off to sleep,
dreaming about the adventures
that tomorrow might bring...

Glittering stars sparkling bright,
Ribbons of colors lighting the night.
Ice and snowdrifts, fox and hare,
This is the home of the Polar Bear.